CHIAMAKA OKIKE

Seeri

"Maybe my relationship - was like my years as a political artist, unavoidable, something that had to be undergone. And I have to believe that love, like that work, was not wasted."

TIM KREIDER, I WROTE THIS BOOK BECAUSE I LOVE YOU

Contents

Acknowledgments

Seeri is a testament to when an immovable object (staunch perfectionism) collides with an unstoppable force (tight deadlines). I've always believed that anything worth doing is worth doing with community, and that being said there are a number of people I need to thank for this novella defying an age old physics law and existing.

I would firstly like to thank my parents for replying 'of course!' When I told them I wanted to be a writer, those two syllables have powered me through my entire life.

I would like to thank my most long standing beta reader, Toluwalope Ayoka, for being the person that I want to tell all my stories to, fiction or otherwise. Every character I've ever written would love you too (except the losers).

Thank you to Damisola Sulaiman, for both the friendship and the proofreading. For always having the right words and being the foundation where I can build the emotional interiority of myself and my work.

This novella would not be possible without the help of Seyni Abdoulaye, for grounding me, supporting me, and bettering me in every imaginable way. I'm counting down the days till we replant our hibiscus bush.

To Alero Oyinlola who demanded that I write a longer body of work, congrats, you won! You'll always hold the title of president in my fan club, and best believe I will forever be the president of yours.

To Gabrielle Emem Harry, the third Gemini on this list, you understand my words and I understand yours and there's nothing I've written since I've known you that has not been better for you reading it.

Subomi Ige, the world's best project manager, event coordinator, and professional talker downer from a ledge. Thank you, for keeping my head on my shoulders and being the reason my dreams see the light of day.

To all my friends who picked up frantic, stress induced calls and sat with me as I poured over every minute detail, thank you! To Somina Daminabo, for being the sun. To Temi Chukwumah and Atinuke Awo for hilarious and grounding commentary, to Mofehintoluwa Olugbemi for her endless nodding and 'yeah's' on the phone. To Jordaine for beta reading the novella in record time. To Vanessa Aboagye for listening to me *complain* about writing the novella in record time. To Osahon Ize-Iyamu and Mubarak Dawodu for the part time role they took up as my cheerleaders. To Deji and the Hotel Zamara team for being on the receiving end of my strictness, thank you for allowing me to be a part of the beautiful thing you've created.

I hope this story is a legacy of all the miraculous and tumultuous relationships that inspired it. Truly, love is never a waste.

Thank you for reading a happy story, and making *me* a happy writer. Here's to joy (which I hope you felt) and to its enduring power of creation.

SEERI

Kewa startled, spilling a rose pink liquid across the counter and onto the mauve of her toenails. Within seconds Tajudeen was at her feet with a paper towel, dabbing away the liquid.

"He's at King's Cross now!" She shouted, accidentally pouring even more of her drink onto the floor and into Tajudeen's hair.

Tajudeen grunted at the same time that Kewa gasped.

Upon realising what she had done she hoisted Tajudeen up to her eye level and reached for a new paper towel, gently patting away.

"Shit, sorry!"

"It's fine." Tajudeen soothed.

"If we get a taxi we can be there in 40 minutes." Kewa continued, still distractedly swiping.

Tajudeen grabbed both her hands and lowered them slowly.

1

"Kewa, you don't even know where he's going."

"He's walking on Pentonville Road." She pressed her finger against the dot on the screen that represented her ex-boyfriend. "There." She said again, pressing harder to illustrate her point as the dot took rhythmic leaps forward.

Tajudeen eyed the phone up and down.

"Okay," she inhaled slowly, "and?"

"And Tobi lives there!" Kewa shuffled across the counter, shoving lip-gloss and her house keys inside a blue saddle bag, all the while balancing her cup in her hand. "It's his 24th today, he's probably still throwing the party he told me about and-" she turned away disconcerted as the dot on her screen made a particularly big leap. "Makin is going to be there." She finished.

"Have you wished him happy birthday?"

"Who?" Kewa asked absentmindedly.

"Tobi, listen-" Tajudeen grabbed Kewa by the waist to steady her. When they were facing each other, Tajudeen began smoothing her hand down her solar plexus and didn't stop until Kewa started doing the same. "Good." She removed her hand from Kewa's waist. "Now, let's say Makin *is* there. Do you know who else is going to be there?"

"Tobi?"

2

Tajudeen frowned.

"Well *obviously*, but who else?" She pressed.

"Zandi maybe, who cares?"

"Zandi, and Miracle, and Imoteda and Monique." Tajudeen listed off her fingers. "Put the drink down for a second and *think*, Kewa. What exactly is your plan here?"

"Just to-" she said and flailed her arms.

"Mhm? Just to what?"

Kewa inhaled and as Tajudeen requested, set her cup down on the counter top. She placed her hand back on her chest, rubbing the same spot in circular motions until she felt her heartbeat slow. It was a small ritual that Nijah had invented. It was a ritual she had shared with Makin. She shook her head as if to drive off the thought and stepped backward until she was on the other side of the kitchen island.

"I know that this is impromptu. I'm not trying to bail on our night."

Tajudeen waved her away.

"We can drink wine on any other night, it's not about that. What do you want to do?"

"I'm not sure." She said softly and glued her eyes to the corner

3

of her toe where her nail polish was chipping.

"It's a year tomorrow."

"I know."

It was Tajudeen's turn to drop her drink. She circled around the counter until she was facing Kewa squarely again.

"What do you want to do?" She asked again.

"It's just that... She knew him. And she liked him. And she would have wanted me to do *something*."

"Yes but," Tajudeen faltered, "would she have wanted it to be this?"

"She was a romantic."

"She was delusional."

"Exactly."

Tajudeen sighed and scrubbed a hand over her face. If she weren't so frustrated she might laugh at the familiarity of the situation. It was unnerving how similar the sisters were when they argued. She shifted her fingers away from her eyes so she could get a better look at Kewa's face. Across it she could see the artifacts of Nijah. She and Kewa used to have the same dimple on their chin, but Kewa's had filled out the older she got. Right then Tajudeen wanted to press her thumb into it, hoping it would leave a dent so that for a moment she would be staring at her best friend's face again. She kept her hand by her side because she knew that the illusion would only last a moment. If she looked any longer, she would see that Kewa's bottom lip was a startling pink colour, a sharp contrast to the darker rosewood of Nijah's. Or that Kewa's long eyelashes pointed downwards, opposite to the short, north facing lashes that framed Nijah's eyes. And even though it wasn't the kind of thing one could know by just looking at someone, Tajudeen would remember that Kewa's baritone voice sounded nothing like Nijah's falsetto one. The differences were stark in Tajudeen's mind, but it was only because she'd spent a lifetime studying them, committing their distinctions to memory. Making a note of every time Kewa asked for cherry flavoured lollipops where Nijah had requested strawberry. Or the way Nijah would boil the milk that she added to her cereal and Kewa would add ice cubes to her cerelac bowls.

When Nijah died, people had pointed to Kewa as a salve for Tajudeen. They had told her to take comfort in the fact that Nijah wasn't *really* gone. They would cite the grey streaks in Kewa's otherwise jet-black hair, Kewa's lopsided strut, and the way Kewa's nose leans slightly to the left as all the evidence that her best friend was still alive. And for a while Tajudeen leaned into it. It was easy enough to do because Kewa spent months not speaking. And in that silence, Tajudeen could craft her into whatever she needed her to be. But the quiet didn't last forever, and the first time she heard Kewa's laugh after the funeral, her masterpiece of delusion fell apart at the seams. She remembered being in swimming class with Nijah at 10 and their instructor adding a h in front of every instruction to breathe 'in' and 'out', and how they had to dip their heads under water to hide their giggles. Or how they had bought and drank a full bottle of vodka at 14, and Tajudeen had gotten so drunk that she clung to the walls and begged them to stop moving and Nijah literally screamed with amusement. Or when they were 19 at their first funeral together and the pastor had described Mrs. Ogunsola- a notorious witch and tormentor- as a 'God fearing, kind, and well-loved member of the community' and Nijah had whispered 'na wa' under her breath and gotten them both kicked out of the chapel for cackling. When Kewa laughed, it sounded nothing like any of the times that her and Nijah had laughed. And it was the first time Tajudeen realised she would never hear the sound again.

But she also realised, after not hearing it for 17 weeks, that she liked Kewa's laugh. And even though it confounded and worried many other people, she liked Kewa's silence. She liked Kewa entirely. She didn't *need* Kewa to be Nijah. But in that moment, the way her eyes shone with determination as she tracked the green dot across the pixelated map, Tajudeen was transported to the first month after the funeral when all she could see in Kewa was grey streaks, lopsided walking, and a left leaning nose. Maybe it was her three quarters gin and one quarter grape juice drink that had just kicked in, but she felt hopeful again. She looked down at her phone and saw that it had just turned 12:00. Officially a year since Nijah died. She took a deep breath and locked eyes with Kewa.

"Okay. Book the taxi."

As the tiara of the bride-to-be fell into her lap for the third time in five minutes, Tajudeen realised her decision had *definitely* been fuelled by the three quarters gin and one quarter grape juice drink. Thus far the only thing making their shared taxi bearable was the mini bottle of rum that one of the bridesmaids had pulled from inside her boot and passed to her and Kewa to drink. She had waved it away, but Kewa had finished it in one unflinching gulp.

"When's the wedding?" Kewa asked the woman in the pink veil, pink sash, and matching pink tiara, roughly wiping the back of her hand against her mouth.

"Watch your lip-gloss, guy." Tajudeen said at the same time as the bride-no-longer-to-be sniffled "I called off the wedding."

She and Kewa let out a simultaneous "oh," and shared a panicked glance.

"This is an anti- bachelorette party!" Her friend declared, "because we don't need slimy, cheating, capri sun straw spined men as husbands."

Kewa widened her eyes as Tajudeen scratched the back of her neck. Even their driver averted his eyes in the mirror.

"Out of curiosity do you have any more of that rum left?"

Tajudeen asked eventually.

She was handed a bottle from a woman who introduced herself as Maanhitha, the ex- maid of honour. Together her and Gemma, the runner up for the maid of honour position, shared with Kewa, Tajudeen, and the taxi driver the story of how a Mr. Gary Wright had been having a torrid affair with the florist for months leading up to the wedding.

"And the worst part of it is, we go to church together!" The bride, who over the course of Gemma and Maanhitha's story had been revealed to be named April, wailed from the front seat.

Tajudeen and Kewa weren't generally unsympathetic people by nature. However, in that moment they both simultaneously recalled how Nijah was a notoriously dramatic crier. As April howled and turned a spectacular colour of red up front, both Tajudeen and Kewa remembered how Nijah had once strewn her entire body against a concrete floor because she was upset that a concert she had been waiting months for had been cancelled. Every new theatrical sob from April sent both girls closer to the precipice of unrestrained laughter. When April fisted her hair in her hands and jerked back and forth in the passenger seat, they took turns looking out of the window and pointedly avoiding eye contact.

Oblivious to their repression efforts, Gemma turned towards Kewa and Tajudeen for a reaction.

"Very un-Christlike of her." Kewa humoured her.

"A Jezebel, if you will!" Tajudeen chimed in.

"And it took me so long to catch on because it wasn't suspicious that his clothes smelled of flowers. I thought he was just being a good husband, rightfully invested in the wedding." April sniffled.

"We should have known," Gemma shook her head dramatically, "no man on earth gives a damn about the perfect hibiscus flower hybrid." She framed the last phrase in theatrical air quotes.

Suddenly, the laughter disappeared in Kewa's throat. She locked eyes briefly with Tajudeen before averting them to focus her eyes on the upcoming streetlights. Hibiscus was Nijah's favourite flower even though she had never seen one in real life. They'd read about them in one of their father's many encyclopaedias and had promised that when Nijah was 25 and Kewa was 24 they would visit Nigeria for the first time together and pick hibiscus flowers from their grandmother's garden in Abeokuta. Their grandmother died when Nijah was 22 and Nijah had followed the year after, so in the end Kewa was 23 and had still never seen a hibiscus in real life. Makin had made an effort though. Because she'd once told him about Nijah's fixation on the flower, after the funeral he had brought her a fridge-load of handmade zobo that he and Tobi had brewed the night before. Back then she was still unable to talk, and in the absence of words both the relationship and the zobo had spoiled. Tajudeen had tried one before the rest of the batch went sour. She said they needed more sugar but that it was still a solid attempt. She had rated it a 6.5/10.

9

And that's why Kewa couldn't drink it. Because she and Nijah were supposed to fly to Nigeria in first class together, drinking champagne instead of orange juice on the flight for the first time. Kewa was going to pick a random blockbuster movie that would have been trending that year but that she'd never gotten around to watching. Ten minutes into the movie Nijah would start pulling off her headphones and demanding that Kewa give her attention. And she would have obliged, and they would have spent the 6-hour flight in innocuous conversation about designer heels, the latest reality television show, and the first food they would try when they landed. On the drive to Abeokuta, Nijah would have fallen asleep on her, and Kewa's shoulder would have started to cramp, but she would have stayed still for the 1.5-hour trip anyway just to let her rest. She and Nijah were supposed to exchange looks when they met family they hadn't seen since they were babies. At night they were supposed to laugh together about how Aunty Ronke had shouted at Kewa to 'remove that ṣẹẹri stick from your mouth' lest her teeth rot. And how Aunty Kayin had wrapped a scarf over Nijah tank top because 'this your breast is too much.' In the morning, they would tell their grandmother how much they wanted to try zobo, how they had never had any their whole lives, and how it came from their favourite flower. The last bit would be a lie because Kewa's favourite flower was actually the one that sprung from the Venus fly trap plants. When Nijah went to piano lessons or dance classes, Kewa would read the encyclopaedia with Tajudeen. The day that they stumbled on the page about the Venus fly trap plant, Kewa had grimaced and tried to flip away but Tajudeen had held the book open, pointing at the small drawing in the corner.

"Let's look at someone else, this one is yucky." The six-year-old Kewa had moaned.

"No, look." Tajudeen had coaxed, tracing her hands over the small white petals. "It's beautiful."

It had made Kewa pause to study it. She looked from the wiry stem to the oak brown of Tajudeen's eyes. She looked from the green that framed the white to the bright red of Tajudeen's thumbnail. She tilted her head and looked at the entire flower, pretty and delicate, laminated on the page. Then she looked at Tajudeen, who was smiling and looking back at her; and she agreed, it *was* beautiful.

Still, Kewa would have committed to her and Nijah's plan, waiting excitedly at the lunch table as their grandmother brought them zobo that she had sent her live-in house girl to buy from across the street. They would have poured it into the big metal cups that were offered to them, clinked their drinks together while making unblinking eye-contact, and taken a sip of a perfect drink. It might have been bitter, it might have been too sweet, it might even have been just okay. But she would have been drinking at home with her sister, the sun beating mercilessly down their back, laughing as they inspected one another's faces for their initial reactions. It would have been a 10 out of 10, so why would she settle for less?

Tajudeen, noticing her friend's mood change, placed a comforting hand on her knee. Or at least it was supposed to be her knee, but the alcohol made her misaim and her palm ended up flat against Kewa's upper thigh. Kewa, unmoved by the placement, layered her hand on top of Tajudeen's and began tracing the ridges on her fingers.

"That's enough bitching and moaning from us." Gemma chastised. "See," she gestured at Tajudeen and Kewa, "there's still real love out there."

Tajudeen and Kewa shared a brief glance, suppressing the laughs that threatened to burst out of them.

"How long have youse been together then?" April snivelled from the front.

"Uh, actually-" Tajudeen started, getting ready to correct them.

"It must be three or something years now." Kewa started. She leaned into Tajudeen and shifted her arm so it fell across her shoulders.

"I didn't think they were a couple." Maanhitha commented, mostly to herself.

"We don't always know if it's safe to be." Tajudeen responded.

"Oh no we're safe." April nodded enthusiastically. "My cousin is a lesbian and I was at her wedding last year. She beat me to the altar, I guess." She said and took another swig out of her mini bottle.

"And *I* was a lesbian in uni for a few months. Had a girlfriend and everything." Gemma cut in again

12

"Oh *my*, a whole girlfriend?" Kewa asked with mock sincerity.

"She cheated and I fell in love with a different man." She pulled down her dress so they could see the cross tattoo on the left side of her chest.

"Hallelujah," Tajudeen turned towards Kewa, "I think?"

Kewa lifted and raised her shoulder in an "I don't know' gesture.

"I'm bi." Maanhitha added.

Tajudeen and Kewa sent her enthusiastic nods of approval.

"What about you then?" April asked, turning her chin defiantly towards the driver, who up until then had sported a nearly inconspicuous smile. "Are you homophobic?"

"Why? Because I'm black?" He asked without taking his eyes off the road.

April began sputtering a response that was disrupted by the sound of Tajudeen and Kewa giggling into their hands.

"I'm joking," he clarified, after half a minute of watching April squirm in her seat. "I'm taking my partner to the Arsenal match tomorrow. It's our 7th anniversary and he's never seen a game. So no, *not quite* homophobic."

"Who are they playing against?" April asked.

13

"Chelsea." He groaned. "If Arsenal loses, I have to do the dishes for a week."

"Hope you've stocked up on Fairy?" Tajudeen quipped.

"If I had known you were a Blues fan, I would have declined the ride." He responded.

"This season has been great for us! Chelsea has been-" Tajudeen started, eliciting a groan from everyone in the car. She rolled her eyes and raised her palms up in surrender, leaning back into her seat.

"See, even your girlfriend hates them." He shrugged.

"You don't hate them, do you, girlfriend?" Tajudeen leaned into Kewa to ask in her most saccharine voice.

"I love whatever you love because you love it." Kewa responded in a voice equally caked with sarcasm.

"Do you mind me asking how you met?"

Because the alcohol had started taking root in her, Kewa wasn't sure whether the question had come from Maanhitha or Gemma, but she answered anyway.

"It was at uni. I studied theatre and she was in the room when I was auditioning. The play that year was Hadestown and my scene partner had bailed on me. When she saw me practically breaking into hives on the stage, she started reading out the lines for me from the audience. But for a second, I didn't realise that she was reading out the lines, so when she said that thing." She snapped her fingers trying to remember. "Yes, that line that goes 'all I've ever known is how to hold my own, and now I want to hold you' I froze because. Well, because she said it with such conviction that I forgot that she was acting. And I'm the same way since my sister-" she paused as her breath caught in her throat. She felt Tajudeen's fingers press into her shoulder. "She was older, but she was also a dreamer, and very delicate. She was good at being held. And maybe because I was younger, I thought I had something to prove so I became tough, or at least I tried to be. That audition was a... hard time. I'd been, you know, holding things together for a really long time, but standing there in that auditorium was the first time that I felt like I could fall apart."

"Love at first line?" Maanhitha asked.

"From the moment I saw her." Even though Kewa was responding to Maanhitha, she twisted her body so that she was making eye contact with Tajudeen. In response Tajudeen released a tight smile.

* * *

Tajudeen *had* been in the room the day of Kewa's audition, but she'd lingered behind the curtains, deathly afraid of climbing onto the stage. So instead, she had watched from the sidelines as Makin, from the audience, recited the lines to Kewa, as Kewa froze momentarily and then sprung into action, and as Kewa fell in love.

Kewa had told the story of that audition day a thousand times. But she'd only ever told the other story, the one about the night before, to Nijah. Tajudeen had been helping her rehearse tirelessly for weeks, stopping by after her shifts at an American candy shop with cherry lollipops and a printed screenplay in hand. That particular night, perched on the side of her bed with a tongue coated in bright red, Kewa had asked Tajudeen to kiss her.

"Ew." Was Tajudeen's succinct response.

Kewa launched a pillow at her.

"What do you mean ew? Stand up and kiss me, jare."

"Why would I do that?"

"Because Orpheus kisses Eurydice."

"Other way around actually."

"Tajudeen, get up."

"Has anyone ever told you that you might be *too committed* of an actress?"

"I'm passionate."

"You're insane."

"I promise it's not..." She faltered when Tajudeen looked at her. She had been faltering when Tajudeen looked at her for weeks now. It had started as faint bells, tolling gently when Tajudeen smiled at her from across the lunch table. Then violins when Tajudeen pushed a forkful of pasta into her mouth while making unflinching eye contact. Then a base that reverberated through her whole body when Tajudeen held her hand. One day, after they had been practising particularly late, Tajudeen hugged her goodbye, and while her head was buried in the crook of Kewa's neck she whispered a soft goodbye that made the choir kick in. Now they were inches away from each other, Tajudeen having finally obliged, and there was an entire orchestra roaring behind her ears. "It's not anything." She completed.

Tajudeen nodded wordlessly.

"What's my line again?"

"That's good." Kewa answered.

And with that Tajudeen stepped even closer, hovering milliseconds away from Kewa's face. She leaned in quickly, in one big push, and suddenly Kewa was on stage. It was the largest auditorium in the world and a thousand spotlights were pointing at the two of them, the music had crescendoed, and the crowd had risen to their feet in rapturous applause. It was perfect melody and it was blinding light, and she couldn't believe that somehow, in a single moment, the two of them had managed to create the world's greatest spectacle. It was strange because Kewa had done this before. She had lived so many other lives. At 10 she had played a weeping and amorous Juliet.

17

At 15, Elinor, as she was torn between sense and sensibility. Her most recent stint was playing both Catherine and Heathcliff in a gender-bending one woman show, and even that didn't compare. But then again, what could? She'd lived in the greatest love stories of all time, pretending she knew what it meant when Juliet said

My bounty is as boundless as the sea, my love as deep; the more I give to thee, the more I have, for both are infinite.

Or when Jane Austen wrote

my heart is and always will be...yours.

Even screaming the words from the centre of a stage, tears streaming down her face, pretend pining as a distraught Catherine, she never believed they could be true. That she could ever feel that

"If all else perished, and he remained, I should still continue to be; and if all else remained, and he were annihilated, the universe would turn to a mighty stranger."

But then Tajudeen pulled away, Tajudeen tucked a loose braid behind her ear, Tajudeen stared bluntly at her, and suddenly there was no pretence anymore. There was no stage, no spotlights, no sound. There was just her, Tajudeen, and the taste of cherry, tucked into a 7ft by 10ft uni bedroom. And it still, somehow, managed to be unequivocally *spectacular*.

"It isn't finished." Tajudeen said.

"What?" Kewa had asked, dazed.

"That's the next line." She took a step back from Kewa. "It isn't finished."

♦

"I think I need to throw up." April shouted suddenly.

Kewa, having just relived the memory of Tajudeen stepping away from her, felt similarly. She settled instead for leaning forward, placing a hand on April's shoulder because it was what her alcohol-soaked brain recommended as a useful course of action.

"Right, I'm pulling over." The driver announced, swerving smoothly on to the side of the road.

Because Tajudeen was the closest to the door, she was the first to step out. She caught April in her arms as she poured out of the front seat. When she buckled under the weight and tumbled to the floor, Kewa came rushing out of the car with Maanhitha and Gemma in tow. They collectively scuttled towards the nearest bush, all the while murmuring platitudes to April about how it would all be okay. The sound of her vomiting into the fauna was overshadowed by the screeching of tires as the driver rapidly pulled away.

"Son of a-" Maanhitha started, only to be cut off by April shouting

"My sash was in there!"

The women looked amongst each other, each varying levels of disgruntled.

"What now?" Gemma asked.

"Tobi's is still like 40 minutes away." Kewa responded.

"Who's Tobi?" April drawled from where she lay on the ground.

"Tobi," Tajudeen grunted, "is someone who doesn't matter right now." She sent Kewa a hard look then stepped away so she could see the entire group. "Okay does everyone have their phones?"

Everyone, even a still doubled-over April, nodded.

"Keys?"

She was met with nods again.

"ID? Shoes? Purses?"

The group nodded in near unison once again. Tajudeen pulled out her phone and went silent for a few moments.

"Right," she spoke up suddenly, "we're a 9-minute walk from the closest store and we need to get April some bread and water. We're going to go over there, call a new taxi, and rate this last guy a one star, okay?"

"Okay." The group concurred.

9 minutes quickly transformed into 17 as April took a break to sit on the concrete and complain about her aching feet. She then proceeded to throw her strappy pink heels into the street, causing a passing biker to fall onto the side of the road and adding another 7 minutes to their journey.

"Do you guys sell cigarettes?" April boomed as she walked through the door of the off licence.

The man at the till didn't have a moment to recover as Gemma bounded in after her.

"I thought you quit smoking?"

"You also thought you were going to be a bridesmaid to a wedding in a week." April picked a can of beer from the open fridge and pointed it towards Gemma. "Things change."

Maanhitha wrestled the beer out of her hands and replaced it with a bottle of water.

She grabbed April by the hand and manoeuvred them towards the back of the store, scanning the aisles for bread.

"Just these two." Kewa placed two bottles of water on the till. "Oh, and this too please!" She added a cherry lollipop to their bill. "Do you want one?" She turned towards Tajudeen questioningly. When Tajudeen nodded and pointed towards the grape, she turned back towards the counter, pushing their order forward.

"Card please."

It took 6 minutes and three tries to get April to sit upright, but eventually all the women collapsed onto the concrete floor with bottles and bread in hand.

After a few moments of collective deep breaths, sighs, and muttering, Maanhitha turned towards Tajudeen and Kewa.

"Have you guys called a new taxi?" She asked.

Tajudeen held up her phone as a response.

"Two minutes away." She replied.

"I bet you can't wait to get away from us." Gemma teased.

"A little." Kewa admitted, to which Tajudeen elbowed her.

"That's fair enough." April said her first word in 10 minutes. "If I was around a psychotic ex-wife, or ex-bride or whatever, I would want to leave too."

"Oh no, I didn't mean-" Kewa started apologetically.

April waved her away.

"It's okay, love. I'm self-aware enough to know that I've been a misery to be around tonight. I've probably been a misery for a few weeks." She rested her elbows against her knees. "The wedding was supposed to be in Brighton, you know. But I

22

had always planned for the hen do to be in London, and it's stupid but I didn't want to give up everything about the wedding and... And everything about the relationship with Gary." She spat on the ground as if his name had left a bad taste in her mouth. "He was supposed to have his Bachelor's party tonight as well, and we were going to meet at a hotel in Mayfair at 3:00am to compare notes on our day. Whoever threw up had to buy breakfast for the other person the next day. We had to toss in a mimosa as well if either party got on top of a table or took off an item of clothing." She stopped to look at her bare feet for a moment. "I don't know if shoes count, but anyway." She looked up suddenly and towards Kewa and Tajudeen. "I know you don't share the same, you know," she thrashed her arms, "*sentiment*, or what not. But it really was lovely meeting you. You're both funny, and proper cute. And it's always nice to get a reminder that love isn't always a complete waste." She spat on the ground again as if love too had left a bitter taste.

"It's never a waste at all," Maanhitha replied, "and we love you."

"Yeah, we do." Gemma nodded emphatically.

"You're just saying that because I'm buying breakfast tomorrow." April shook her head, smiling slightly.

"If you can even *lift* your head tomorrow." Gemma added.

"Oh, she's definitely getting breakfast with us tomorrow. Mimosas and everything." Maanhitha replied as she pointed at April's feet. "Shoes count."

23

* * *

As they waved goodbye from their new taxi it occurred to Kewa that she hadn't checked her phone in nearly an hour.

"Shit." She swore loudly.

"What is it?" Tajudeen asked, alarmed.

"I still haven't wished Tobi a happy birthday."

"Oh shit. Just quickly text him and then put him on your story."

"Saying what?"

"ML, bro."

"Be serious."

"More blessings."

"Tajudeen." Kewa deadpanned as her friend fell over with laughter into her lap.

"Just say happy birthday, Kewa."

Kewa turned her attention towards her phone, typing furiously for a few minutes.

"Okay, done!" She declared and sunk into her seat.

"If that was hard, what are you going to say when you see Makin?"

Tajudeen felt her sink even deeper into the seat.

"Hey." She said,

Tajudeen looked up at her.

"Hi," she responded.

"Yeah, that's about it."

"I wouldn't take you back if I was him, not gonna lie."

Kewa groaned loudly and buried her face in her hands.

"Are you okay over there?"

"I'm not good at love confessions," Kewa moaned, shaking Tajudeen's arm, "help me."

"What makes you think *I'm* good at love confessions?"

"I just feel like no one can be worse than me."

"You're an actor, steal a line or something."

"No!" Kewa groaned. "It has to come from me, it has to be real."

25

"What? Then why were you asking me?"

"Because whatever souls are made of, yours and mine are the same."

"Okay, if that's the sort of stupid shit you were planning to say to him, I see why you needed a second opinion."

"Exactly!" Kewa fisted her hands through her hair. "Okay what's the most romantic thing someone has ever said to you?"

Tajudeen frowned.

"That they liked my... *smile* or something."

"Who said that?" Kewa asked, scratching her head. "Wait, I*'ve* said that to you."

"And I thought it was romantic." Tajudeen shrugged.

She felt Kewa stiffen.

"Did you actually?"

Tajudeen felt tension snake its way through her body until it settled like lead on her tongue.

"No, I-" Tajudeen started, stumbling over every syllable. "I know you wouldn't- I know you didn't-"

"What? Compliment you?"

"Obviously you compliment me."

"But you don't think I mean it?"

"No, I just know *how* you mean it." Tajudeen said as she lifted herself from Kewa's lap.

"How do you think I mean it?"

Tajudeen shifted uncomfortably.

"What will you say to Makin?" She asked, speaking more to the seat belt than Kewa.

"That-" Kewa perked up suddenly as her phone vibrated in her bag, "Oh, Tobi just texted back."

"What did he say?"

"Thnks sis! C u."

"24 years and he still refuses to type full sentences." Tajudeen shook her head. "What did you end up sending?"

"Nother 1 round d sun! Congrats on lvlling up, big 24!"

"Kewa?"

"I'm kidding, I just said happy birthday with three hearts and told him that we're 15 minutes away."

"Fair enough." Tajudeen replied, and they fell into a silence that wasn't entirely comfortable. "Okay, I'm not very romantic so disclaimer," she started, "but the" she cleared her throat. "The reason I liked the compliment about my smile or whatever, was because it made me feel like you," she was talking slowly, leaving a pause between every word.

"Tajudeen, talk with sense abeg." Kewa grunted impatiently.

"Na wa," Tajudeen laughed to herself. "It's because it made me feel like you know me. You didn't just say you liked my smile; you said you could sit in my cupid's bow." Tajudeen looked away. "Which doesn't even make any sense. But you're always saying things like that. Like you could walk along my palm lines-"

"Because I've memorised them."

"Or that you could make a cake recipe from my scent."

"You wear vanilla perfume!" Kewa retorted defensively. "And in winter you use coconut oil as a moisturiser."

Tajudeen was going to point out that she had only started using coconut oil this winter. Before then she had been a Shea butter devotee until sometime last November when the skin on her lower back became inflamed and Kewa knelt for ten minutes massaging coconut oil into her. That same day she'd massaged the rest of Tajudeen's back, pressing into every knot until it gave way. When she had finished with the massage, Tajudeen perched in between her legs as Kewa pulled her hair into a tight bun. She sat still as Kewa tinkered around her face, obeying her every instruction to open and close her eyes. Kewa nodded or shook her head from the bed as Tajudeen held up different outfits. Before Tajudeen left the house, rushing towards the bus station with her heels barely buckled, Kewa had pulled her back to kiss her cheek.

Tajudeen remembered the date she had been preparing for that night going relatively well. They'd had dinner at an Italian restaurant that had chairs wrapped in fairy lights. It was quaint, beautiful even. But throughout the night Tajudeen felt Kewa's hands running across her spine. She thought if she reached for her back then she would feel craters in her skin where Kewa had touched her. And it wasn't just her hands she could still feel. The bright, citrus perfume of Kewa wafted into her nose as she ate. When the waiter came to ask if there was anything that they needed, even his voice reminded her of Kewa. Not because of the way it sounded, but because of what he'd asked.

"Do you need anything?"

And Kewa was nothing if not the essence and the answer to the question. Kewa was always asking her 'do you need to rest?' And presenting her bed. 'Do you need to eat?' And leading her into the kitchen. 'Do you need a place to stay?' And opening up her arms to be stepped into. Tajudeen said to the waiter what she had said to Kewa every time the two of them were together and she asked if there was anything else Tajudeen needed.

"No. This is everything."

She also added a thank you, obviously- because she had home training.

♦

In the car, Tajudeen's nose filled with Kewa's bergamot and citron fragrance as she inhaled deeply.

"You are a strange one." She shook her head.

"I know."

"But."

"But?"

"Someone loved you for it. Someone *loves* you for it. So just, I don't know, say that kind of thing to him. It might sweep him off his feet."

"Did it sweep *you* off your feet?" Kewa asked, making a show of batting her eyelashes and hovering seconds away from Tajudeen's face.

"Like I said," Tajudeen turned her head so there was only a sliver of distance between their lips, "I'm not a romantic."

* * *

Tobi managed to topple both Tajudeen and Kewa to the floor

when he spotted them. He smelled of musk and liquor as he wrestled them into his arms.

"Big 24!" Kewa giggled from the ground.

"The biggest." Tobi concurred as he wrapped his arm around Kewa's and lifted her.

"Are you good down there?" A passerby in a mini black dress and burgundy boots asked as she hovered over Tajudeen.

"Not particularly." Tajudeen muttered, adjusting her top and keeping her gaze deliberately fixed on it.

"Let's get you on your feet then." The stranger offered, outstretching long, manicured nails that matched the burgundy of her boots.

As Tajudeen looked up, Kewa saw her friend's eyes brighten slightly, and upon becoming eye level with her rescuer, explode with light.

"I'm Vivian." She presented, still holding on to Tajudeen's hand.

"I'm Kewa." She interjected, shaking Vivian's free hand.

"I'm Tobi, and it my fucking birthday!" He whooped.

None of the women looked towards him. All eyes were zeroed in on Tajudeen who still hadn't said anything since she was on the floor.

"I, uh, thank you." She said eventually, unlinking their hands. "I'm Tajudeen."

"Say again?" Vivian asked, leaning so Tajudeen's mouth was by her ear.

"Tajudeen." She repeated more loudly.

Vivian nodded and leaned back so they were making eye contact again.

"Isn't that a boy's name?"

"My dad was very disappointed when *I* was what came out on November the 8th."

"Oh, you're a Scorpio?"

Tajudeen nodded.

"News that disappointed my father even more than me being a girl."

At Vivian's raised eyebrow Tajudeen explained further.

"My mum was an amateur astrologist in uni, that's where they met."

"I'm a Sagittarius." Kewa interjected.

"No way," Vivian smiled, "me too! When's your birthday?"

"It's-" Kewa's answer was cut short as she spotted Makin at the drinks table, pouring a shocking amount of gin into a red cup. "Something I'll have to tell you later. Sorry, excuse me." She weaved past the two of them and bee lined to the table.

* * *

"No." Makin responded.

For a moment, Kewa stood dumbfounded, staring at her ex-boyfriend whom she had just asked to speak to, and who had responded with the two-letter word she'd dreaded the most and expected the least.

He spent a few more moments taking in her slack jaw and furrowed eyebrows before breaking into a grin.

"I'm just kidding." He reached for her hand and began guiding them towards the balcony. "How far?" He asked, when they settled in the corner. As the door shut behind them, she felt her ears ringing with the sudden silence.

She shook her head no when he offered her a joint. He shrugged and lit it up.

"How far?" He asked again.

"I'm," she started, smoothing her hands down the front of her top. "Let me take you up on that offer actually." She said and outstretched her hand.

"That's new." He commented as she exhaled.

She shrugged.

"Taking after my sister."

He frowned briefly but didn't respond. They were guided into a momentary silence that Makin was the first to break.

"What are you doing here, Kewa?"

"Smoking."

"Kewa."

She exhaled deeply.

"I wanted to come talk to you."

"And say what?"

She thought about it for a moment. She wanted to tell him that she'd started adding purple streaks to her braids because it was both Nijah and Tajudeen's favourite colour. She'd gone to a night time only fun fair for the first time in her life three weeks ago, and she wanted to tell him about that too. About how when she sat on the Ferris wheel, she'd thought about launching herself off of it, but Tajudeen had placed a steadying hand on her thigh. Or she could take him even further back to when she'd gotten a flu shot and cried when she saw the needle and Tajudeen had held her jaw and turned her head away until the doctor announced that it was over. How she hadn't even felt the pain, just the indentation of Tajudeen's fingers. She had taken on embroidery as well; she thought that might be worth mentioning to him. Every Sunday evening, she would sit on the couch with Tajudeen curled below her and they would listen to a podcast about philosophy or fashion or true crime. Sometimes they would just sit in silence.

Which is what she actually came to say to him. That she was sorry for her silence. For months after Nijah died, she didn't utter a word. She didn't say good morning to her mum, she didn't say 'excuse me' to strangers on the road as she weaved past them, and she didn't say 'I love you' to Makin. Which was another thing she had come to apologise for. She wanted to explain that she understood how talking was important. Her and Nijah could spend endless hours enraptured in discussions about the meaning of the colour blue, whether they believed God was real, and who they might be if their father was in their lives. Sometimes it felt like all they did was talk. She understood, logically, how senseless her vow of silence was, but she also felt like the only person in the world who had an ear that picked up all the frequencies of her voice was gone. And with that as her truth, there was nothing worth saying anymore.

"Well, I-" she took a breath to steady herself. "I wanted to say that I'm sorry."

"For wh-"

"For everything." She cut him off quickly. "I know that even before… Before she died I wasn't completely there."

"But you're here now."

"I'm… I mean…" She stammered.

He placed a steadying shoulder on her hand.

"Should we… Should we ease into it?" He suggested.

She exhaled deeply and shook out her shoulders.

"Sure."

"Did you finish Desperate Housewives yet?"

"2/3rds of the way through."

"Okay, so same as six months ago."

They smiled briefly at each other, relaxing the slightest bit.

"Are you still going to loc your hair?" He asked as he twisted a braid of hers between his fingers.

"No, but I might dye it."

"What colour?"

"Ginger. How's Dayo?"

"Nice choice, suits you. He's in second year now, passed first year with an 85%."

"Right, so he's still the one that's going to get the family out of the hood."

"Probably. Are you still going to move out of London?"

"Probably not. Are you going home this December?"

"Yeah, me and Tobi both."

She nodded as a response, feeling the air of awkwardness decisively lift. Just as she was about to make a joke about him bringing back zobo for her, she spotted Tajudeen bracketed between Vivian's arms. She tried to turn back towards Makin, but her eyes were trained on the spot where Vivian had placed her hand on Tajudeen's shoulder. She squinted, trying to spot whether Tajudeen had just been laughing or whether it was a trick of the light. She was broken from the trance when Makin placed a gentle hand on her forearm.

"I'm glad you're good, Kewa. But what did you come here to say?"

"I-" her head felt hazy and filled with smoke. It suddenly felt like all the liquor had caught up to her. "So much for easing into it." She swayed slightly and Makin reached out to steady her. "Thank you." She smiled at him. "To answer your question, I came to say that I think I love you."

"Oh." Was his only response. His mouth seemed to freeze around the mouth and Kewa had to fight the urge to laugh at how the space between his lips was a perfect circle. It was closer to a yes than she had been expecting. Which was, she had to remind herself, good news.

"Or, um," she shook her head and gathered her thoughts, "that I definitely love you. When Nijah died, I was so," she laughed humourlessly, "I was so eager to join her, you know? Living just felt so tedious. And then I retreated into this silence and everyone thought I was grieving. But I think I was actually doing that thing that butterflies do? You know with the?" She wrapped her arms tightly around herself. "Sorry, I've had a lot to drink, but you get it. The thing." She wrapped her arms around herself even more tightly.

"A cocoon."

"A cocoon, yes!" She snapped her fingers. "And I wanted to come outside of it as this butterfly," she flapped her arms. "I kind of decided by week two post funeral that I wasn't going to die. Which is kind of fucked up and selfish because why should I get to live and she doesn't?"

"It's not selfish."

She waved him away.

"But anyway, I decided to live. Just so I could have fun stories to tell Nijah when I see her again. But I needed to be in that," she wrapped her arms around herself again, "to get better. To get to a point where I could *actually* do some living. But it was hard. For a lot of people." She tried to swallow but the inside of her mouth was desert dry. "The more people stopped calling, stopped looking me in the eye, and stopped loving me, the more I realised that I was running out of time to get better. So I started eating properly again, and using melatonin and weed to sleep for longer than three hours. And I started talking again and laughing again. I'm better now and... I'm here."

She paused when she saw a flash of movement from inside the house. It was Tajudeen and she was standing alone, scrolling idly through her phone. She must have seen something funny because suddenly her face broke apart into a grin. Kewa's smile followed reflexively after.

"I'm here now, but I return there sometimes."

"To the cocoon?"

"Yeah, there." Kewa responded distractedly. "There." She said again, facing him squarely. "And I realise I love you because you're the only person in the world that can make silence feel exciting. And maybe it's because there's never any real silence when I'm with you. It's like I have bat ears all of a sudden."

"Kewa, you really *have* had a lot to drink." Makin said, half amused, half concerned.

"I really, really have." She laughed. "But I'm getting somewhere I promise. I'm trying to say that silence doesn't feel like silence because I can still hear you. You read me bedtime stories and tweets and your grocery list. I can be halfway to work on the tube and I'll hear your laugh. Even your breathing is familiar. And darkness doesn't feel like darkness because you took me on walks in the sun, and when you slept over you kept the lamp on your side lit, and you yourself, you're-"

She glanced towards Tajudeen who had moved to the centre of the apartment with a drink in hand. She was with Vivian again and she had just said something to make her laugh. As expected, Tajudeen threw her head back too, no doubt cackling at her own joke. Kewa didn't hear the song change but she knew it had because Tajudeen threw her hands in the air and spun Vivian into a circle. When they separated, Tajudeen started her infamous faux break dancing. Her movements were quick and jutted and it made her look like she was stuttering with her full body. It was absurd and it was delightful, and Kewa marvelled at how she managed to be both without spilling even a drop out of her cup.

"Perfect light." She completed. "And when I die, Nijah is going to show me around... wherever it is that she went," her voice broke around the last word. "But I'm here with you in this one, so for now I don't want to see anywhere else."

"You'd postpone a meeting with angels just to hang out with me?" Makin gathered his hands towards his chest, pretending to be moved. Kewa slapped his hands away and smiled.

"No. Let's be serious for a minute about where Nijah ended up."

"Kewa!"

"I'm joking, I'm joking." She raised her palms up. "Just trying to lighten the mood."

"You're ridiculous." He smiled, but it was strained. "I'm happy... That you came to this realisation."

"I mean why wouldn't you be, that was an A star, A level drama love confession."

"It would have kept William Shakes up at night for sure."

"You just said William Shakes unironically but *I'm* ridiculous."

He beamed at her then slowly averted his eyes as his smile faded.

"But it wasn't for me." He smiled again, but his eyes remained distant.

"What? Huh?" She frowned.

"Like I said, I'm happy for you, Kewa." He smoothed his hands down the front of his shirt. "You should tell the person you love that you love them. There's no shame in it. And even if it doesn't go the way you hope it does, I am the best qualified person to tell you that the regret doesn't last."

"Makin, I don't understand."

"So," he started, pausing for dramatic effect, "a few months ago, I told this girl that I loved her. Very fine girl." He winked at her. "Very funny babe too. We met in university at one theatre

41

audition like this. We dated for a *while*, and everyone thought we were going to make it all the way to the altar. I think I believed it as well. I thought that she was it. And she *is* it. She is…" he rapidly fisted and unfurled his hands, "so kind. She's smart as well, she was even the best graduating student in our cohort. She was voted most likely to be rich and famous, and I'm the one who put her name on the ballot. She is so much stronger than she could even possibly realise, but I hate every moment that has made her that. She is… perfect light." He grinned. "It was devastating to not be around her and to not have her, but I'm surviving it. So, I'm going to say to you what my friends, who were sick of watching me cry into my towel in foetal position, said to me."

She looked at him expectantly

"Life na turn by turn."

"What?"

"Life. Is. Turn. By. Turn." He enunciated slowly, rolling the R's.

"Makin." She folded her arms as he chortled at his own joke.

"He told me it was okay, because one day she would be in my position, and she would love somebody, but she would be terribly confused about whether they loved her back. He told me to take comfort in the fact that I'm not a coward, and that when I felt it, I said it, and that's more than he can say for her. We got into a fight that day actually, because I didn't like that he called her a coward. But maybe he was on to something."

He walked over to where she stood and bundled her up in his arms. She returned the hug fiercely.

"Makin," she started.

He tilted his head to where Tajudeen and Vivian stood hip to hip, giggling and whispering into each other's ears.

He placed a hand on Kewa's shoulder and squeezed. For a second, she thought he would pull her closer, but instead he unclenched, spun her around, and took a small step back.

"Prove him wrong." He said from behind her.

She remained rooted in place, not quite believing what he'd said. She reached for the handle of her bag to steady herself. She thought briefly about turning back to beg. He must not have heard her, she decided. She chastised herself for drinking beforehand. It made her thoughts muddled; they must have come out nonsensically. Because if he'd understood her then surely, he wouldn't be pushing her away. He would recognise that it was him. It had to be him. He was the only person who had managed to put up with her for so long. He was the only one to ever *ask* her to be a girlfriend instead of introducing her as that to a stranger one random day after four months of knowing each other. He was the only one that had ever celebrated Valentine's Day with her. He made a big deal out of it every single year, building up the size of the bouquets until in their final year together, the flowers could barely fit through her door. He'd met her mother. He'd met Tajudeen. He'd met *Nijah*. Her sister had made jokes about how she would officiate their wedding *and* be the maid of honour. The three of them had gone to the cinema together, they'd sat in parks for hours talking, when they went on their honeymoon tour around Europe, Nijah was going to join them for their last stop in Italy. They had plans, all three of them. They had a *future*. The last threads of what her life was supposed to be had pulled themselves taut on that balcony, weaving patterns of naming ceremonies and mortgage repayment plans. Then just as quickly, they had all come unravelled. She was starting over, and she was devastated.

From where she stood unmoving, she saw Tajudeen's features contort into one of pure concentration. Her tongue hung from the side of her mouth. Kewa had seen this face twice before. Once was at a fresher's party where the bouncer had to carry Tajudeen on his shoulders and into a taxi at the end of the night. The second was on one of their night outs with Nijah where they had misheard French strangers offering them apple cider and had instead chugged mouthfuls of absinthe.

Tajudeen was about to attempt a split.

She was halfway to her friend before she realised it. When she reached Tajudeen, she grabbed her by the shoulders and steered her away from the circle that was forming. There were shouts of protest, but Kewa ignored them as she led the two of them to the only part of the wall that didn't have bodies crushed against it. As they settled into the corner a passerby knocked into Tajudeen, pushing her body until it was inches away from Kewa's.

"What the hell!" Kewa shouted, whipping her head around wildly to spot the stranger.

"Easy, tiger." Tajudeen soothed, placing a hand on Kewa's chest.

"I'm okay." Kewa responded, breathing heavily.

"Oh, wow he really pissed you off, your heart is *beating*."

"I just hate when men," she didn't complete her sentence.

"Exactly." Tajudeen nodded. Her eyes scanned the room. "Speaking of men... where's yours?"

Kewa shook her head as a response.

"Hug or shot?" Tajudeen asked.

"Both."

"Okay stay here," she instructed. Moments later, she emerged from the crowd with a white paper cup.

"Thank y-," she stopped abruptly as she brought the cup towards her mouth, "wait is this all alcy?"

"Bottoms up."

"No."

"If you want that hug, you're going to have to work for it."

"This is coercion."

"This is companionship." Tajudeen said with mock purity, creating a heart shape with her fingers.

Kewa grimaced as she poured the cup down her throat.

"Urgh!" She yelled after she swallowed.

"You go girl!" Tajudeen laughed.

"You disgust me."

"Aw, you're the love of my life too." Tajudeen said into her ear as she enveloped her into a hug. Kewa found herself dissolving into it. She buried her face into the crook of Tajudeen's neck, exhaling slowly. "You're okay." Tajudeen soothed, gripping her tighter.

Kewa lifted her head slightly to look around the party. Makin had left the balcony. She wasn't sure where he had gone. She submerged herself back into the scent of coconut oil and vanilla.

"Yes," she whispered "I am."

* * *

Tajudeen leaned against a wall, watching Kewa as she moved.

She felt like she was seeing her through a screen. All the other bodies next to her were coming in and out of focus, only she remained, swinging her arms wildly in the middle of the dance floor. Tajudeen felt her breathing constrict when a man in a plaid jumper and wide leg jeans tapped Kewa's arm gently. She watched as Kewa tucked her hands into her pocket, half listening and half swaying to the music. Eventually he smiled and stepped away from her, and Tajudeen's lungs expanded again.

"You're not going to finish that are you?" Kewa approached her, wiping beads of sweat off her forehead.

"Probably not at this rate." Tajudeen responded without looking away from her drink.

"Do you want it in the picture?"

"What picture?"

"There's a photo booth round the corner. You missed it as well?"

"Apparently."

"That's what the guy was asking me."

"To take pictures?"

"Yeah."

"But," Tajudeen frowned, "you don't know him, do you?"

47

"I think that was his way of moving to me."

"How strange."

"How romantic." Kewa countered.

Tajudeen grimaced as a response.

"Come on, come take pictures with me." Kewa tugged her arm.

"Is this your way of moving to me?" Tajudeen teased.

"Of course not, I'm way more smooth."

"I can't," Tajudeen's expression turned serious. "I'm waiting for Viv. She's the one who brought us here, it would be somehow to just disappear."

Even though she had just defended it, she wasn't sure she knew exactly where *here* was. She had pockets of memories from earlier of security dispersing Tobi's house party due to noise complaints, then of the group loitering on the streets talking over each other, then of a voice yelling at full volume

"What's the next motive?!"

To which Viv had responded saying that she knew a place. Thus, the two of them and Kewa had all entered the underground station desperately drunk and stumbling into the central line tube. They alighted at Notting Hill Gate, walked a few minutes, and now her friend was across from her, luring her towards an alleged photo booth.

"Ah, speak of the devil." Kewa pointed as Vivian appeared.

"Hi, sorry, a girl in the bathroom hasn't gotten a text back since Wednesday so I was dealing with *that.*"

"Did you tell her to block them?"

"Well, the last text she sent was her confessing she had cheated so..."

"So, *no.*" Tajudeen smiled lopsidedly. "Do you want to join us at the place?" She simulated a picture being taken with her hands. "Me and Kewa are-"

She paused when she turned towards a stone faced Kewa. Vivian looked between the two of them.

"No, I'm going to join my friend upstairs for a minute. Shout me when you're done."

Tajudeen nodded and faced Kewa again.

"Ready?" She asked.

"Yeah."

As they settled into the chair, the photographer introduced himself as Dumisani and told them that they had four shots. They both sent him a thumbs up at the same time, then giggled at their synchronicity. All the laughter died in Tajudeen's throat and she felt bile rise in its place as Kewa pulled out a gold compact mirror. It was Nijah's. When she was alive, she and Tajudeen were notorious photo booth addicts. Over the years they had collated a total of 122 physical pictures together. All of them were stored in a purple box under Tajudeen's bed. Nijah had bought the mirror at 8 years old, developing a ritual from early on to inspect her face extensively before any photo of hers was taken. Sometimes she would delay photographers for up to five minutes, fiddling with one corner of her lip, or one of her edges that teased itself out of place. In response Tajudeen had learned to start working in tandem with the mirror to speed up the process. She would run her eyes over Nijah's face, inspecting whether lipstick had stained her teeth or if her precise centre parting had shifted even a centimetre out of place. After the far-reaching adjustments were made, Tajudeen would often make eye contact with the exasperated photographer to offer an apology. Privately, she'd always wondered why her friend bothered with such a comprehensive scrutiny of herself when there wasn't a day in all the time that Tajudeen had known her that she didn't look-

"Perfect."

Tajudeen found herself saying to Kewa

"What?" Kewa lowered the mirror.

"You look perfect." Tajudeen clarified.

Kewa froze with the mirror halfway to her lap.

"That's new."

"Is it?"

Kewa recovered quickly, fixing her face so it was neutral instead of twisted in confusion like it was mere moments ago.

"It is. Save it for your babes." She joked.

"We ready?' Dumisani called.

Kewa sent him a nod of approval and posed.

"You look perfect." Tajudeen said again.

The flash went off as Kewa turned to Tajudeen incredulously.

Tajudeen shrugged as a response.

She had to fight herself not to say it for the third time. Kewa had a beauty that made Tajudeen understand why photographs were invented.

"Tajudeen, be serious." Kewa pressed.

"I *am* being serious."

The flash went off again.

"Why would you say something like that?"

"Because I mean it?"

"No." Kewa shook her head "Not with me." She insisted.

"What? What does that even mean?"

The flash went off for the third time.

"Let's not do this."

"Wait, what? Look at me."

Tajudeen pulled Kewa's jaw towards her.

"No," she waved her away, "and stop spoiling my picture."

"The pictures will be fine. Kewa, are you upset at me?"

"No. I just want to get at least one good picture."

"You look-"

"Don't, Tajudeen! Don't say I look perfect, don't hold my face again, don't lean in just so you can keep," she took a deep breath and lowered her voice. "Keep leaning away. Just stay still, and let's take one. Good. Picture."

The flash went off for the final time.

♦

"Someone missed their happy meal." Vivian commented as she approached a sulking Tajudeen.

"Go dance and leave me alone." Tajudeen shooed.

"And miss this delight?" She gestured at a doubled over Tajudeen who had just lifted her head out of her hands to look up. "What's the matter, love?"

"I'm half drunk, I have a headache, and my friend has picked tonight for an impromptu audition of dancing with the stars."

"Damn," Vivian frowned, "that wasn't funny *at all*, you really must be out of it."

When Tajudeen didn't react, Vivian smiled and scooted into the booth with her.

"What's actually the matter, Tajudeen."

"Oh wow, not my government."

"Serious names for serious discussions." She turned towards her. "Come on, get to talking. What's the point of friend zoning me if I don't get to be your friend."

"I didn't friend-" Tajudeen started.

"You did, and it's okay." Vivian laughed. "I'm guessing by the way you keep looking at the dance floor and grinding your teeth that your sulking has something to do with Kewa? That's her name, right?"

Tajudeen nodded.

"Right." Vivian tilted her head as she watched Kewa move, "what did you do to get that angel mad at you?"

Tajudeen sighed deeply. Like Vivian, she slanted her head as she examined Kewa's movement. Watching her then it felt like her heartbeat wasn't confined to a single organ. She could feel it thumping in her chest, but it was also ricocheting in her skull and knocking at the base of her spine. It wasn't the first time Kewa had made her feel like this, but the novelty of the feeling never seemed to dissipate. She closed her eyes and waited for the sensation to pass. She had taken to jokingly calling them symptoms. She'd kept track of them over the years, making a note when a new one emerged.

She didn't understand what was happening to her body the first time her feelings manifested physically. They had been 10 years old playing pretend. Kewa was the rich socialite wife and Tajudeen played her seven-figure earning lawyer husband. It had taken hours to convince Tajudeen to participate and when she finally did, Kewa was overjoyed. She talked Tajudeen through every scene leading up to their marriage: the meet-cute that was Tajudeen colliding into her on the street as she held a stack of books, their first date that was in a makeshift couch fort that Kewa said was actually a five-star restaurant, and their first kiss that was under the pouring rain. She wasn't sure if Kewa had planned for it or if she was just fast on her feet, but the second it started to drizzle she hoisted a protesting

Tajudeen into their back garden.

"Kiss me!" The young Kewa had commanded. And when Tajudeen hadn't immediately obliged, she was comforted by Kewa with the fact that "It's not serious."

That was the first time she felt her throat tighten around itself, pushing air away from her lungs so it felt like her chest was inflamed.

Then they were 14 and Kewa had just come back from her first ever real date with a dreadlocked white girl. She collapsed into Tajudeen's bed with tears pooling in her eyes, recounting how the Lisa or Lydia girl had tried to kiss her, and she'd run away. Tajudeen had taken Kewa into her arms, soothing her with platitudes about how she doubtlessly looked like a movie heroine as she ran away in her long pink skirt. Kewa's mortification gave way to laughter which then gave way to an epiphany as she launched away from Tajudeen's arms and instructed her friend to teach her how to kiss because she'd never done it before. When Tajudeen pointed out that she had done it before, that *they* had done it before, Kewa reminded her that they were children, that it was pretend, that it wasn't anything sincere. And Tajudeen had kissed her then because she wanted that kiss to count. She wanted to beat Lisa or Lydia. She wanted to beat everyone. She wanted to be the only person that had ever kissed Kewa; and she wanted it to be real.

When Tajudeen pulled away to look at Kewa that day, it felt like her stomach was a tapestry. Like the knots kept on tying and tightening around themselves the longer she looked at Kewa.

Years later, as Kewa flipped through the Hadestown script, she looked up briefly to say words that were all too familiar to Tajudeen. Followed by words that were all too devastating.

It's not anything.

It had been lifetimes since their last kiss, and this time Tajudeen was prepared. She let Kewa's words roll over her in waves, making sure that they settled into the pit of her stomach. It was with this weight that she walked towards Kewa reciting the words she had said to herself a million times. Words like fantasy, words like pretend, words like nothing at all. Her bones turned liquid as she walked towards Kewa, the first time they had done so. It was all she could manage to stay upright and look her friend in the face, reminding herself of what this moment was and wasn't.

It was nothing at all when Kewa was so close to her face she could smell the cocoa butter she'd smeared on her lips. It was nothing at all when she buried her hand into the crook of Kewa's neck and pulled her impossibly nearer. And it was nothing at all when she leaned in to kiss Kewa and the taste of cherry exploded in her own mouth. It's nothing at all that sometimes, when Tajudeen looks at Kewa for long enough she can still taste the red. And how the flavour coats her life, how all her days with Kewa are drenched in corn syrup and carmine.

How Kewa makes

Everything
  Everything

Everything

Sweet.

♦

"I ruined her pictures." Tajudeen confessed.

Vivian raised a single eyebrow and smirked as she watched Tajudeen watch Kewa.

"Is that all you did? To your *friend*, I mean."

"I don't know why you said it like that but yeah. That's the summary."

Vivian hummed quietly.

"Hm okay," she flexed her fingers. "How would you feel about me taking her to the photo booth to cheer her up?"

Tajudeen shot up in her seat.

"What?"

"The photo booth." Vivian repeated. "If she's upset about her pictures, don't you think she deserves a do over?"

Tajudeen ground her teeth.

"I mean, I guess so." She shrugged.

"Might ask her to brunch tomorrow as well," Vivian continued. "Bacon grease should help with the hangover."

"She doesn't get hangovers." Tajudeen said loudly. She cleared her throat and lowered her voice. "And she doesn't eat bacon."

"That's helpful." Vivian nodded enthusiastically, "anything else I should know? Other dietary restrictions? Favourite genre of music? Oh!" Vivian snapped her fingers, "what's her favourite kind of flower?"

"The little white ones that grow from Venus fly trap plants."

"Hm," Vivian put a finger to her chin. "Those might be hard to source in London. What about her date location preferences? Is she more activity based or a dinner and movie type of girl."

"Activities, but a very specific kind."

"What kind?"

"Well, she liked kintsugi when we tried it."

Vivian bobbed her head again and Tajudeen continued.

"And outdoor activities as well. We did like a whole nature day and created a scrapbook out of it. The goal was to collect items that reminded us of the other person. So, flower petals, interesting shaped leaves, blades of grass we sat on."

"Uh huh." Vivian cocked her head to the side.

"She could do dinner and a movie. We do that sometimes. But we always have to watch it at home because she makes us pause the movie to google the history of each geographical location or the hometown of one of the extras. Random shit like that." Tajudeen caught herself smiling and re-arranged her features so she went back to looking neutral. "It got so bad that for one of her birthdays I bought her a notebook that is specifically for film watching." She tried to restart her explanation in a voice that didn't betray any excitement. "She makes little drawings of stars in the margins. It's kind of become her everything book and she carries it around all the time. She even probably has it now."

"Right."

"Oh, a funfair!" Tajudeen perked up despite her best efforts. "When we were little, we went to this funfair and she fell off the merry-go-round and she's never gotten over it. Till date she still says that's her ideal first date, just so she can re-do the memory." Tajudeen's muted smile had transformed into a full-on beam. "So, if you wanted to take her out," her smile tapered, "um, if you wanted to ask her out, that would be the way."

Vivian eyed Tajudeen for a few moments before bursting into raucous laughter.

"Tajudeen." She let out between wheezes, "you kill me."

"What? What's funny?"

"She's not angry at you because of some picture, she's angry at you because you're a coward."

"Excuse me?"

"And you might also be a little slow."

"Woah."

"She's been shooting daggers at me since I first said hello to you at Tobi's house."

"She wears glasses normally; she was probably just trying to see you better."

"Right, and that also explains why she's turned away the three different guys who've come up to dance with her."

"Kewa doesn't like strange men."

Vivian scrubbed a hand over her face and groaned exasperatedly.

"Tajudeen, it's you."

"I don't understand."

"Yes, that's why I said you're slow." Vivian sighed as she stood up. "I'm going to go ask her to dance, Tajudeen. And I get the sense that that's not okay with you. I get a *stronger* sense that you're not going to do anything about it. But hey, you can prove me wrong. Or you can sit twiddling your thumbs as somebody else goes after the love of your life."

Tajudeen huffed a bitter laugh.

"Kewa doesn't want…" She looked down at her hands, clenching and unclenching her fists. "Kewa isn't the love of my life."

Vivian looked at her unflinchingly for a few moments before nodding once, decisively, and backing away.

"Okay then," she shrugged, "maybe she's the love of mine."

♦

Tajudeen watched Kewa from the corner as she turned a dark blue colour in the light. As the song changed, she transformed into a violet purple and then just as quickly, a soft baby pink. She was facing Vivian, and her head was thrown back in a laugh. The blue light came back again, this time bouncing off her silver chain. Tajudeen studied her for a few moments longer before slowly pulling out her phone and angling it towards Kewa. She took three pictures in rapid succession. She looked at them and frowned.

Too blurry.

She shifted from the wall, taking a step closer to where Kewa danced. She lifted her phone again, capturing the split seconds her friend's face contorted as one song flowed smoothly into the next. She held the screen close to her face, scrolling through them quickly.

Out of focus.

All around her Tajudeen felt the room slowing down. Arms started wrapping gently around shoulders. Bodies that were far apart started moulding into one another. As Vivian tugged on her hand, Kewa smiled politely and unlaced their fingers slowly. Her head whipped around the room; confusion etched into all her features. She stood in the middle of the dance floor, unswaying, with her arms crossed. Eventually, her eyes made one final journey around the room, and she spotted what she had been looking for. In an instant, all her chaos gave way to joy. She unfurled her arms, she let her shoulders drop, and she smiled. Tajudeen's fingers hovered over the capture button, seconds away from a decisive click. She let the moment pass and instead opened her arms as Kewa poured into them.

"I'm not mad at you anymore." Kewa shouted over the music.

"What?"

Kewa tugged Tajudeen through the crowd and pulled her through the door.

"I said I'm not angry at you anymore." She announced as they settled into a corner on the street.

"That didn't last." Tajudeen teased.

"It never does."

"Yeah."

"Yeah." Tajudeen echoed. "I uh, tried to take new pictures. Of you I mean. I felt bad about the other ones that I, you know, ruined."

"Let's see."

They crowded around the screen as Tajudeen scrolled through her photos.

"I like that one." Kewa pointed. "Delete that one, I look crazy."

"You look…" She trailed off.

"Vivian asked for my number."

Tajudeen stiffened.

"Did she?"

"Yeah. She said she'd like to take me to a funfair?"

"You love funfairs."

"I hate them." Kewa countered quickly. "They're the grounds of my greatest defeat."

"Oh."

"I said no, I think I could only ever go to a funfair with you or

Nijah. You're the ones that have to watch me rewrite history."

"Wouldn't it be hilarious if you fell off again."

"No, it would be the last thing I ever do before I go join my sister wherever she is."

They smiled at each other briefly.

"She would hate that joke." Tajudeen said eventually.

"Maybe. But she would love the idea of me falling off the merry-go round again."

"I'm sorry." Tajudeen said suddenly, and Kewa didn't have to ask to know that she was apologising about Nijah.

"We can start to head." Kewa said finally.

"Want me to call a taxi?"

"No, I bought one lemon vodka drink at the bar for £14, it's TFL's time to shine."

Tajudeen frowned.

"But you hate vodka."

"Nijah didn't." She shrugged. "What a lunatic."

"Right. *She* was the lunatic." Tajudeen half laughed, "Let's go home."

* * *

Tajudeen squeezed Kewa's arm as the bus hit a bump. Kewa squeezed back and rested her head on Tajudeen's shoulder.

"You know what's sad?" Kewa said suddenly.

"What?"

"We didn't fulfill any of Nijah's dying wishes."

"She didn't really have dying wishes though, did she? I don't think she was necessarily *planning* to die."

"Well no, but don't you remember all the things she said she wanted us to do before she died? Or if she died."

"The doves released at her wake." Tajudeen said.

"Yes," Kewa raised her head up, "and the way she wanted everyone to have a party pack."

"What did she want in it again? Super malt and chocolate biscuit?"

"*Lucozade* and chocolate biscuit." Kewa corrected.

"Right," Tajudeen smiled softly. "Do you think she would have liked the day?"

"I don't know, but I fucking hated it."

♦

The afternoon of Nijah's funeral was sunny. Tajudeen remembered because she had stopped to take a picture of the light as it poured through green leaves. One of Nijah's death wishes had been to have an outdoor funeral, specifically one in the woods at daybreak. She would have been disappointed to see mourners filing into marble coloured chairs in a small garden at 2pm. She would be even more disappointed at Tajudeen's outfit, an ill-fitting black dress draped over black tights and old black ballet flats. In Tajudeen's defence, Kewa was wearing almost the exact same clothing, even down to black stud earrings. They had smiled momentarily when they spotted each other before Kewa was whisked away by an aunt whose assigned seat had been stolen by one of Nijah's work friends.

It was nearly an hour later before Tajudeen saw Kewa again as she was perched at the edge of the stage, with white sheets of paper held with shaking fingers. Tajudeen's eyes trailed the hem of her dress as she positioned herself in front of the microphone, clearing her throat.

"Hello," she started in a small voice. "My name is Oluwakewa, I was or, um, *am*, Nijah's younger sister. I actually looked up how to write a eulogy because I've never really done one before." She cleared her throat. "First, I'm supposed to tell you about the deceased. Um, her name was Nijah, and she was my sister. She was 5 '8 and a Pisces and she used to go running every Sunday morning when she stopped going to church. I don't know if these are all supposed to be positive, so I added in some negative traits just to give you a full picture of her as a person." She adjusted the microphone. "Nijah used to snore very loudly, if you were sharing a bag of chocolate chip cookies, she would eat the last one and never offer it, and if you're ever going anywhere with her you have to add an extra hour to the actual time of arrival. Or um, had to rather. I'm not sure about the tense of these things." She cleared her throat again. "Some of her good traits included being great at braiding, flirting to get us free drinks, and volunteering at the homeless shelter near our house." She paused as she squinted at the paper. "Sorry I couldn't make out the next bullet point. It says funny anecdote. A funny anecdote about my sister is that one time we went to this underground club place. Me, her and Tajudeen were 3 out of the 7 black people there including the bouncer mind you. Basically, one thing led to another, and Nijah ended up dancing with this compact blonde, white man called Edward. As she was dancing this photographer started hovering around her taking pictures from 100 different angles. On the way home we teased her about how she had an admirer, but we didn't think anything of it past that point. The next morning Tajudeen starts screaming at full volume. Naturally me and Nijah run over to see what she's looking out. Turns out the club had posted pictures of Nijah and Edward dancing but they'd photo shopped Nijah's bum so it was twice the size. They'd also edited my hair and made it a dirty blonde colour."

When the crowd responded in a range of muffled laughs and

gasps, Kewa smiled slightly.

"It was even funnier in person, trust me." She folded one piece of paper under another. "I'm also supposed to talk about the people who meant the most to her, but it felt indulgent to talk about myself. My parents are great. Well, my mum is anyway. Her colleagues are also here, she liked you guys as well." Kewa said and waved to the three women in the fourth row who raised confused hands back. And then there's Tajudeen. I could talk about her, but it would probably be redundant because anyone who loved Nijah loves Tajudeen. Or at least if you knew Nijah then you know Tajudeen." She tucked a loose braid behind her ear, visibly shaking. "The last thing is a quote of hers. Or something she always used to say. If you spent enough time around her you've definitely heard her add 'abeg' to the end of every sentence. But I don't know if that's profound enough to stand out in a eulogy. I don't even know why I'm saying any of this out loud." Her voice had started cracking after every word, and the crowd could hear her hyperventilating into the microphone. Tajudeen stood up quickly and walked towards the stage.

"Hey." She coaxed Kewa from the side.

Kewa's eyes pooled as she looked at Tajudeen.

"Hi," she responded.

"Want me to finish the eulogy?"

Kewa stepped away from the microphone to crouch near where

Tajudeen stood. She shook her head no.

"What, do you think I won't get the inflections right?" Tajudeen joked.

"You never get the inflections right." Kewa giggled as a tear fell onto the front of her dress.

"Fair enough. Do you want me to hold your hand as you finish it?"

"You hate stages."

"This is hardly the West End." Tajudeen glanced at the crowd. "Plus, it's just one more page right?"

Kewa nodded.

"Okay," Tajudeen hoisted herself up, "let's go."

On stage they stood with fingers interlaced as Kewa rounded up the last parts of her eulogy. Tajudeen inhaled slowly, focusing all her attention on the mud stain on her right shoe.

"One day," Kewa started with a shaky voice, "Nijah went to a party with this group of people she'd never gone out with before. It was her first year of uni and she was trying out new crowds. She stormed into my room at like 2am and her pupils were dilated, and she was only saying one word every three seconds. She started ranting about how she had come to this great epiphany about love. She said that love was like a drawer. Or maybe it's the heart that she said was a drawer?" She frowned. "It doesn't matter. The point was that it is made up of all these different compartments and things. She said that the biggest part of love was grace, but she only said that because she was going through an identity crisis and she thought she needed to be forgiven for it. And sometimes she did. I wasn't happy or kind to her when she would barge into my room at midnight after partying, or when she'd walk back into the house wearing clothes she hadn't told me she'd borrowed. But I'd take her now, in all her noise and thievery. And I would take her then too. There isn't a version of Nijah that I haven't loved. I don't know how much I agree with her compartment theory. In everything that makes up love I find her there. I love her in grace, in patience, in adoration, in forgiveness, in humour. Whatever makes us dance to music playing from her phone at 9pm on a Sunday evening, I love her there. Whatever makes us sit, unblinkingly watching truly concerning levels of old Nollywood movies without saying a word to each other, I love her there too. Whatever makes us buy one pack of chocolate cookies instead of two, *knowing* that we will fight over the last biscuit, but looking forward to holding hands once the wrapper is empty, I love her there the most." She untangled her and Tajudeen's hand to wipe her tears away before returning, lacing their fingers together once again. "They said the last part of the eulogy is supposed to be the thank you. So, thank you, Nijah. For giving me the chance to love so thoroughly. I have hated being the girl with the dead sister. I thought that it washed me in something ugly and unbearable, but it doesn't. I've always lived right at your epicentre. And whether grief or love, thank you for allowing me to love you so much that it becomes what I'm known for, and who I am. Nijah Olaitan, survived by Oluwakewa."

Tajudeen hadn't looked up once. Partly because she had been crying so hard she was surprised the microphone hadn't picked it up, and the other part was because she truly did hate stages. Right from when she was little, she would make herself scarce during Christmas productions, insisting that she had a never ending running stomach and locking herself in bathroom stalls. It was where she had met Nijah at 5 years old who, instead of passing over a wad of tissue under the door, had barged into her stall with an entire roll. She'd asked the young Tajudeen a round of rapid-fire questions about who she was and why she had taken up residence in the bathroom. She must have been satisfied with her answer because she left her stall but promised she would be waiting by the door. And she had. Nijah had been at the foot of every door for the past 18 years, pulling Tajudeen through them. She ushered them both through the archways of restaurants, gates of parks, and curtains of photo booths. Each time they were at the precipice of entering somewhere new or leaving somewhere familiar Nijah would put on a coaxing, pleading voice as she asked Tajudeen to walk through with her. Tajudeen would humour her, feigning reluctance. But she always knew, like she had known from the first day Nijah had barged into her life, that there's not a door she wouldn't walk through if her friend was on the other side of it.

She agreed with Kewa's eulogy. Loving Nijah had made her more of all those things; more graceful, more patient, and more adoring of every bit of life. But the thing she thanked her friend for the most, and *loved* her friend for the most, was that knowing Nijah had made her brave. And with that, she took a shaking step towards the microphone, never once averting her eyes from her feet even as she felt Kewa's gaze trained on her. She swallowed so loud that the microphone *did* pick up her sound then. When she opened her mouth to speak, she felt her throat closing at the same time that her knees threatened to buckle beneath her. She took a steadying breath. She shook her shoulders and took another one. She willed herself to remember Nijah. But instead of Nijah at 22 in her signature strawberry blonde braids and silver eyebrow piercing, she saw Nijah at 5, black haired and baby faced. She remembered the stark white of the tissue paper Nijah had shoved into her lap and the way she'd grinned so wide that all 20 of her baby teeth were visible. Tajudeen felt air sneak its way into her throat once again.

"Hello everyone, my name is Tajudeen and… There are party favours in the back. They're in the nylon purple bags so um, grab one on your way out."

♦

"You did well." Tajudeen comforted her.

"I just followed the eulogy templates I saw online."

"Isn't it kind of fucked up that those exist."

"It is." Kewa conceded. "But they did make my life a hell of a lot easier. Don't use one for me though."

"What?'

"A template. For when I die. Don't write a eulogy."

"Do you want me to go on stage and rap?"

Kewa hit her shoulder lightly.

"I don't want there to be a stage at all. I don't..." She sighed without completing her sentence. "I hate that there are things I said about Nijah that she didn't know. I thought that so many things were a given, you know? I was practically born into loving her, so I don't think I ever stopped to tell her how much I liked her. How much I *still* like her. And I don't want anyone else in my life to feel like this. To feel so.., full. But not in a good way. Because now I can spend the rest of my life talking about how fond I am of this person, but the person will never know." She raised and lifted her shoulder. "There's no point.

Tajudeen nodded slowly. She turned away from Kewa as she blinked back tears. She had written a eulogy for Nijah's funeral. In the week leading up to it she had even practised in front of her mum and brother. But when the day came, she kept the pages she'd written folded into three and buried in a corner of her black tote bag. Nobody got to hear about the tissue paper, the open door, and all the lifetimes they lived together afterwards. She didn't get to talk about how funny Nijah was, how astonishingly kind, and how committed she was to adventure even up until her last day alive. Kewa was wrong about pointlessness. Nijah might never know, but she was survived by people who could still listen.

Tajudeen cleared her throat loudly, waiting for Kewa to focus on her. When they locked eyes, she began.

"The first part of the eulogy: telling you about the person."

"What?"

"Oluwakewa Olaitan is a Sagittarius sun, she's 5' 10, and she embroiders on Sunday evenings, even though that's a pretty recent development."

"Are you still drunk?'

"A little, but that's not the point." She placed a finger over Kewa's lips. "Some of her negative traits include: delusion, an over enthusiasm for poorly thought-out plans, and unfounded self-doubt."

"I'm not *that* delusional."

"Oluwakewa also has positives. She's easily charmed and charming, if only one person is laughing in a room it's probably her, and… she's beautiful. I would also like to add that a negative trait of hers is that she hates being complimented even though every good thing ever said about her…" Tajudeen's breath caught for a moment, "is more than justified."

Kewa shifted uncomfortably.

"Next, a funny story. So, Kewa is an actress, but she's also a perfectionist. Before every show she makes me practise lines for hours and hours and *hours*. Obviously, I get bored or tired

74

or both, so I sit down. When that happens, she starts singing my name, like quite literally belting. One day she's on stage and she's reciting her lines as normal. Then when her coworker sits down, before she can stop herself, she starts scream-singing 'Tajudeen' to the entire auditorium. Luckily, it was just a dress rehearsal, but still."

Kewa smiled as she recounted the memory.

"She has this anti-compartment philosophy on love that most days I agree with. It's about how you can find love in all these different places. And I do with her. She's here." Tajudeen moved her right hand towards her stomach. She'd always had a gut feeling about Kewa. "She's here." Tajudeen lifted the shoulder that Kewa was just leaning on. She had a Kewa shaped dent in it from years of taking the long route home together. "She's here." Tajudeen flexed her fingers then placed it carefully over Kewa's. The first time she and Kewa held hands, Kewa was wearing dark green nail polish. For days after, Tajudeen felt like there was a forest growing from the ridges in her fingers. "She's always here." Tajudeen moved her free hand and positioned it over her solar plexus. Tajudeen, before she had met Kewa, weighed 16kg. Where Nijah had muscled into her life, Kewa had weaved. She had nestled quietly but firmly in Tajudeen's chest, making a home of her most vital organ. Now when Tajudeen went to doctor's appointments and stood on scales, she always added a little extra to whatever number the weighing machine displayed. She always considered Kewa.

"The last part of a eulogy is the thank you." Tajudeen declared. "So, thank you, Kewa. For letting me say this to you, and for not making me say it on a stage. You're gracious even to the point of death."

Kewa looked at her for a long time without speaking. She knew that if she put her hand to her chest in that moment she wouldn't feel beating so much as she would feel blows coming in and out so rapidly that it resembled one continuous, decisive thump.

"That was a lot for someone who is not a romantic." Kewa raised and lifted her brows. "Do you mean all that?"

Tajudeen thought of a quip but it died on her tongue the second she locked eyes with Kewa.

"I.. I do."

"Are you going to lean away again?"

"Are you planning to lean forward?"

"I asked you first."

"Very mature." Tajudeen teased.

"Answer the question."

"No." Tajudeen's voice turned serious. "I'm not."

"Oh." Kewa's face contorted in surprise.

"What?"

"I kinda thought you would. I was just going to hover close to your face for a little bit and see how long it would take for you to run."

"Well, I'm not running. Are you?"

For a moment it felt like air had been syphoned from her lungs as the question hung between them.

Kewa thought about what it meant to survive somebody. For a while she had worn Nijah as second skin. Before each day she would drape her sister over herself, going to nightclubs on the high street because that was where Nijah liked to spend her Friday nights, ordering calamari and shrimp at every restaurant she visited because Nijah was a seafood fanatic. But it got tiring, and miserable, and life increasingly became a thing she wanted to weave herself out of. Until she was with Tajudeen. Tajudeen, who coaxed her out of heels and shrugged her out of mini dresses. Tajudeen, who spent countless evenings in her kitchen making her hand-drawn pasta and lemon chicken. Tajudeen, who let her sit in cocoons, and sit in the same position for hours, and sit in silence, and sat with her. Tajudeen, who pushed her existence to the very edge. She made her feel every single inch of the word survive. No, she made Kewa feel every single inch of the word *alive*.

"No," Kewa shook her head. "I'm here."

Tajudeen took Kewa's jaw in her hand to pull their faces closer. She trailed her finger over Kewa's face, dipping her thumb into Kewa's chin for a moment. She smiled when she pulled away and there was the slightest indentation. Her smile widened when Kewa bit down on her jaw and the temporary dimple disappeared completely. When she locked eyes with Kewa she tasted the familiar red.

"In my eulogy," Tajudeen whispered into what was left of the space between them, shifting closer so their shoulders and thighs were pressed against each other, "will you survive me?"

Would Kewa sit in the orchestra that made up Tajudeen? Would she let her feet dangle off the island as Tajudeen whipped around the kitchen? Would she draw new sketches in the margins of the book Tajudeen gifted her? Would she stand in the centre of stages, smiling at Tajudeen as she burrowed herself into a seat in the crowd? She would for the Tajudeen she met at 4 years old, a lanky child with crooked teeth. She would for the Tajudeen she'd known as a teen, when their glasses and braces bumped against each other as they leaned in for their second ever kiss. She would for the Tajudeen she knew a year ago, just before Nijah died. But the Tajudeen in front of her had cut her hair into short blue finger waves from a spiralling afro. She'd gotten a tattoo down her spine and across her shoulders. She was still quick to joke but slower to laugh, and sometimes her smile seemed to stop halfway to her eyes.

◆

Kewa placed a trembling hand against the side of Tajudeen's neck and pulled, bringing their foreheads together. She conjured her very first image of Tajudeen, wearing a white and red plaid skirt and loitering by her door unsure if she could enter. She would never forget the way the young Tajudeen's eyes had lit up when Kewa had smiled and bobbed her head, inviting her in. She would *never* forget. She leaned away then, just the slightest bit, until there was enough space between them to look Tajudeen in the eye. Same light. Kewa nodded then like she had so many years ago and pulled Tajudeen's face close once again.

"I'm here."

About the Author

Chiamaka Okike is a multi-disciplinary writer. After putting it off for years she finally got round to taking her writing seriously. This has led her to editing Isele magazine's women issue, speaking at various workshops and panels, and delving into creative non-fiction - with words and appearances in *The Kalahari Review, Narratively, Wilson Quarterly, Edinburgh's Literary Salon, Brittle Paper, Isele Magazine, ActiveMuse* and her personal website - www.chiamakaokike.com. She is based in London, UK.

You can connect with me on:

◉ https://www.chiamakaokike.com

𝕏 https://x.com/Chiamakaokikee

Also by Chiamaka Okike

Chewed Glass
Chewed glass is a limited short story collection revolving around Wazila.

Return to the Sun
This personal essay explores the evolution of my understanding of love, identity, and belonging through the lens of my fascination and fixation with Biafra.

Perihelion
Perihelion is a heartfelt story told through the last will and testament of Zuo, a person chosen to sacrifice their life for the protection of their village. As Zuo prepares for their fate, they reflect on their unfulfilled desires, especially the love they shared with their best friend, Tariemi. Through tender memories and final requests, Zuo reveals the weight of duty, the pain of letting go, and the beauty of a single kiss that gave meaning to their life.

Printed in Great Britain
by Amazon

59493211R00057